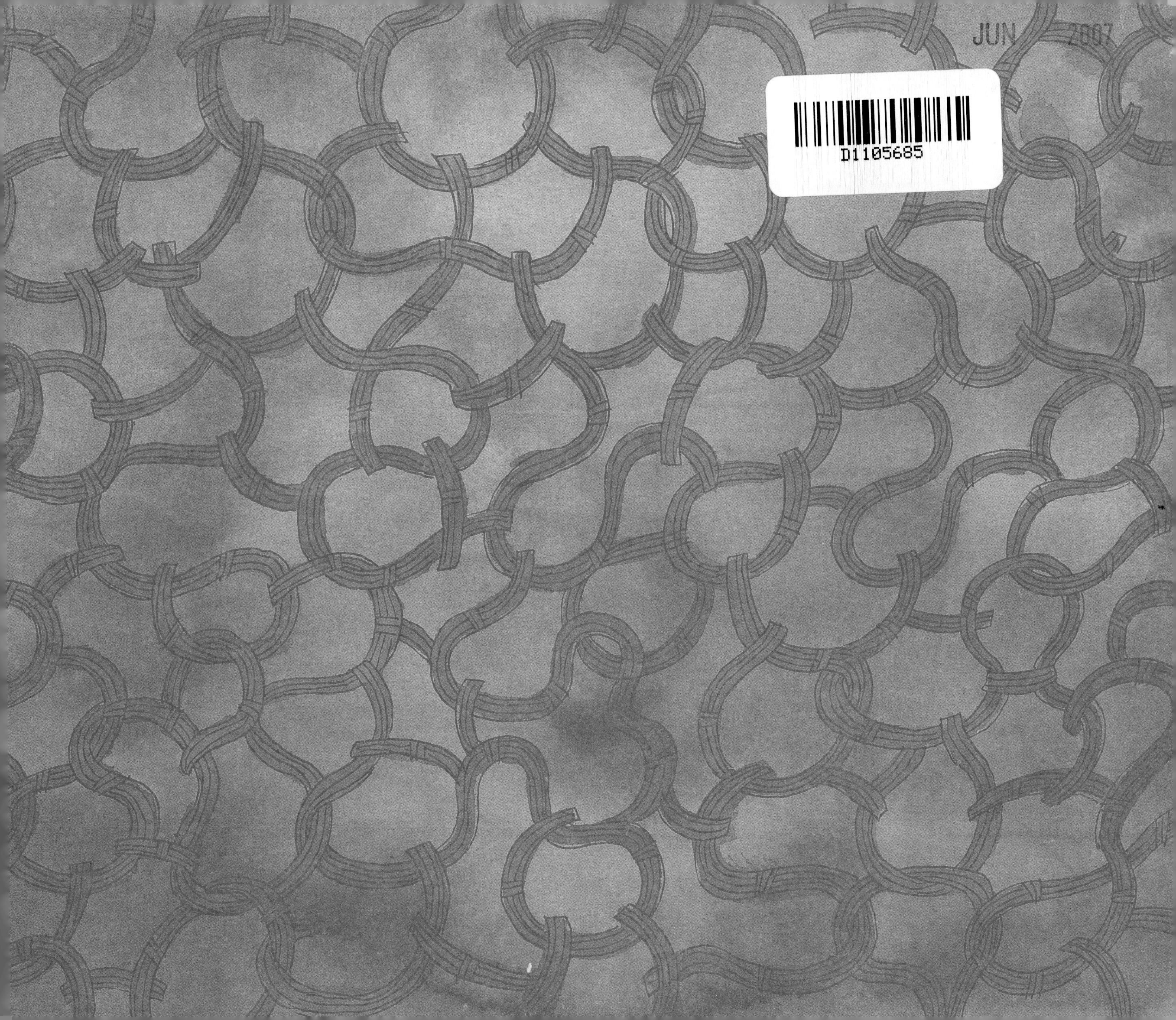

MAUI AND THE SUN

A Maori Tale · Retold and Illustrated by Gavin Bishop

NORTH-SOUTH BOOKS · NEW YORK · LONDON

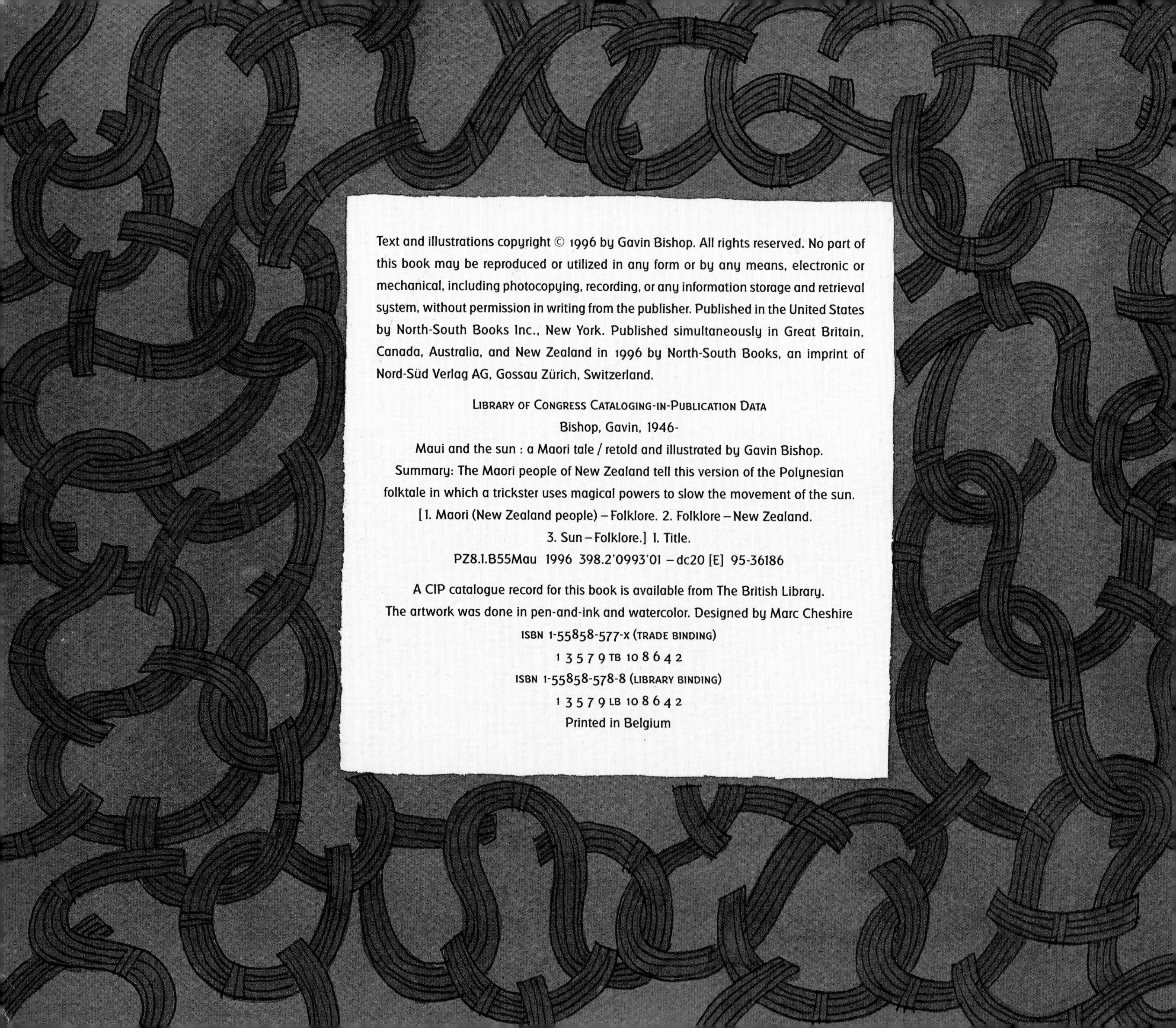

 Published in the United States by North-South Books Inc., New York. Published simultaneously in Great Britain, Canada, Australia, and New Zealand in 1996 by North-South Books, an imprint of Nord-Süd Verlag AG, Gossau Zürich, Switzerland.

LIBRARY OF CONGRESS CATALOGING-IN-PUBLICATION DATA
Bishop, Gavin, 1946-
Maui and the sun : a Maori tale / retold and illustrated by Gavin Bishop.
Summary: The Maori people of New Zealand tell this version of the Polynesian folktale in which a trickster uses magical powers to slow the movement of the sun.
[1. Maori (New Zealand people) – Folklore. 2. Folklore – New Zealand.
3. Sun – Folklore.] 1. Title.
PZ8.1.B55Mau 1996 398.2'0993'01 – dc20 [E] 95-36186

A CIP catalogue record for this book is available from The British Library.
The artwork was done in pen-and-ink and watercolor. Designed by Marc Cheshire
ISBN 1-55858-577-X (TRADE BINDING)
1 3 5 7 9 TB 10 8 6 4 2
ISBN 1-55858-578-8 (LIBRARY BINDING)
1 3 5 7 9 LB 10 8 6 4 2
Printed in Belgium

Yes indeed, Maui was a trickster all right. He played tricks on his older brothers all the time. They were not always pleased with his tricky ways, but they could not help but admire him, for Maui did some pretty amazing things.

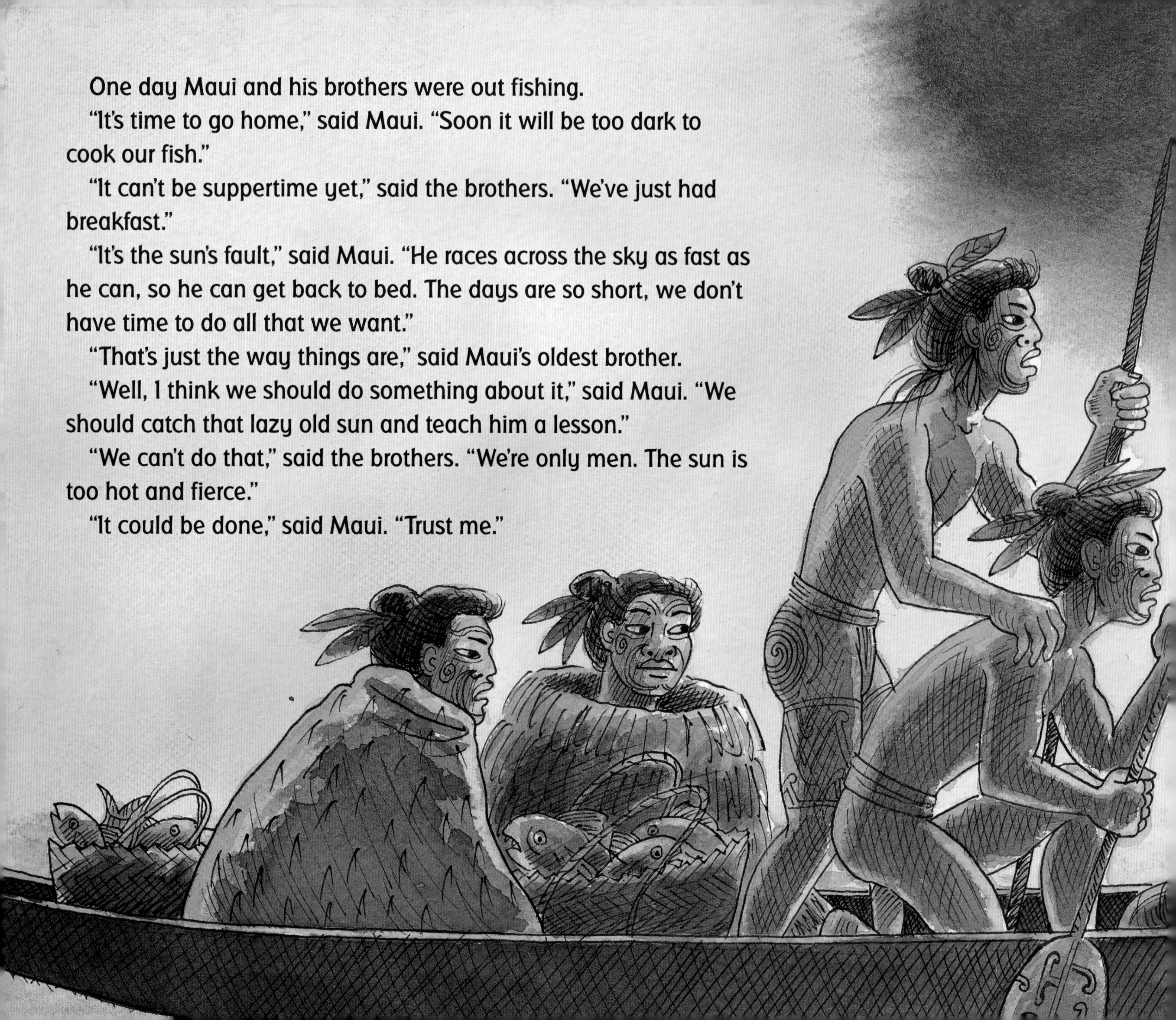

One day Maui and his brothers were out fishing.

"It's time to go home," said Maui. "Soon it will be too dark to cook our fish."

"It can't be suppertime yet," said the brothers. "We've just had breakfast."

"It's the sun's fault," said Maui. "He races across the sky as fast as he can, so he can get back to bed. The days are so short, we don't have time to do all that we want."

"That's just the way things are," said Maui's oldest brother.

"Well, I think we should do something about it," said Maui. "We should catch that lazy old sun and teach him a lesson."

"We can't do that," said the brothers. "We're only men. The sun is too hot and fierce."

"It could be done," said Maui. "Trust me."

And so saying, he turned into a wood-pigeon and flew up into a nearby tree.

"All right, all right," the brothers said. "We've seen your tricks and magic before, but catching the sun is impossible – even for you, clever little brother."

Maui flew back down to the ground and changed back into himself. "Trust me," he said once more.

By the time Maui and his brothers got home, the sun had set. They were very angry that they had to cook and eat their fish in the dark.

"Perhaps capturing the sun and teaching him a lesson is not such a foolish idea after all," thought the brothers.

The next morning Maui told the people of the village his plan. They were eager to help. For days everyone worked in the swamp cutting flax until Maui said, "Stop, we have enough. Now let me show you how to make this flax into strong ropes."

So they made all kinds of ropes. Thick rope, square-shaped rope, flat rope, and twisted round rope.

When they had finished, the ropes were tied into bundles. Maui took up his enchanted weapon – made from the jawbone of his grandmother – and he and his brothers set out towards the east. They traveled only at night, so the sun would not see them on his daily journey across the sky.

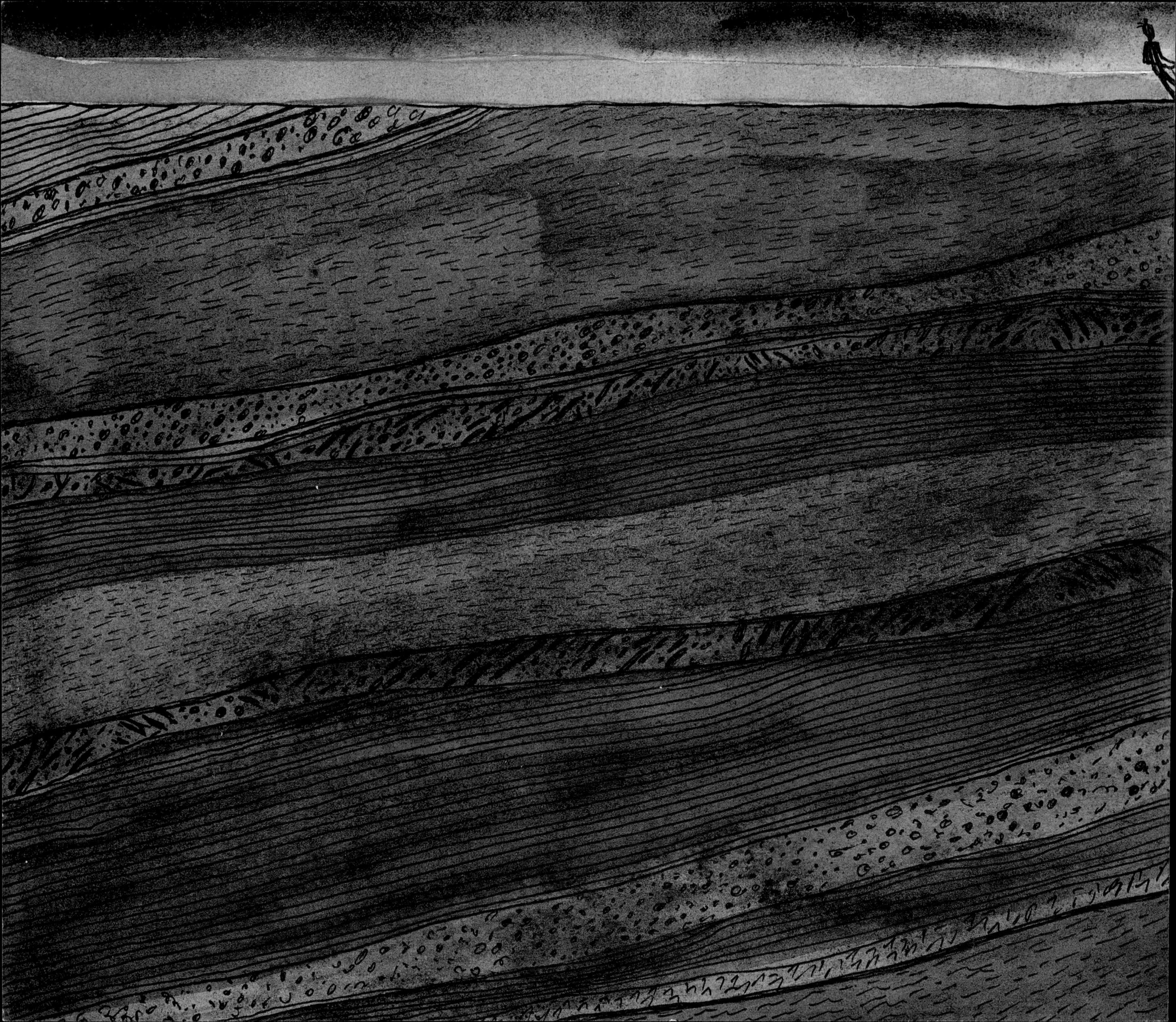

After many weeks they arrived at the edge of the pit where the sun slept. They set to work at once, moving as quickly as they could in the dark. They built a long wall of clay and four huts made of branches. They used the flax ropes to make a huge net. Then they set the trap. Maui made his brothers hide in the huts while he crouched behind the wall on the western side of the pit. Quietly they waited.

Suddenly, from deep down in the earth, there was a shudder. The small huts where the brothers were hiding trembled and shook. The air became hot, and the mist at the mouth of the pit disappeared with a hiss. As the earth heaved, a crack roared along the clay wall where Maui hid.

The sun came slowly out of his pit, suspecting nothing. His rays touched the mountaintops and his fire danced on the sea. Rocks exploded from the heat. Maui and his brothers watched in awe as the sun rose into the flax-rope net, which tightened about him.

"Hold him now! Pull hard!" Maui roared to his brothers. The ropes jerked tight.

The enraged sun screamed and tossed back and forth. He heaved and strained and tried hard to bite through the ropes. Some snapped and fell away. Others caught fire, but most held fast. The little huts burst into flames and collapsed into heaps of ash, but Maui and his brothers pulled even tighter on the ropes.

Then Maui sprang from the shelter of the wall, and with his enchanted weapon, he beat the sun as hard as he could. The sun cried in agony and begged for mercy.

"Why do you treat me like this? Why do you want to hurt the great Tama nui te Ra?"

When Maui heard the sun's secret name, "Great Son of the Day," which was previously unknown to mankind, he gained the power to make the sun go more slowly across the sky.

Mauì gave the signal and the ropes were loosened. The sun feebly pulled himself from his pit and gingerly rose into the sky. That day he set out across the heavens very slowly indeed.

Maui and his brothers returned home and went fishing. Now they would have plenty of daylight to catch all the fish they wanted.

But Tama nui te Ra crept so slowly that he did not return to his resting place for many months. During this time of constant daylight the land became dry and parched. The people were tired because it was hard to sleep.

One day during that time, when Maui was tending his garden, he held up his hand to block out some of the sunlight. The sun burnt him, and Maui rushed to the sea to cool the pain.

Seeing a chance to trick Maui, the sun suddenly decided to set.

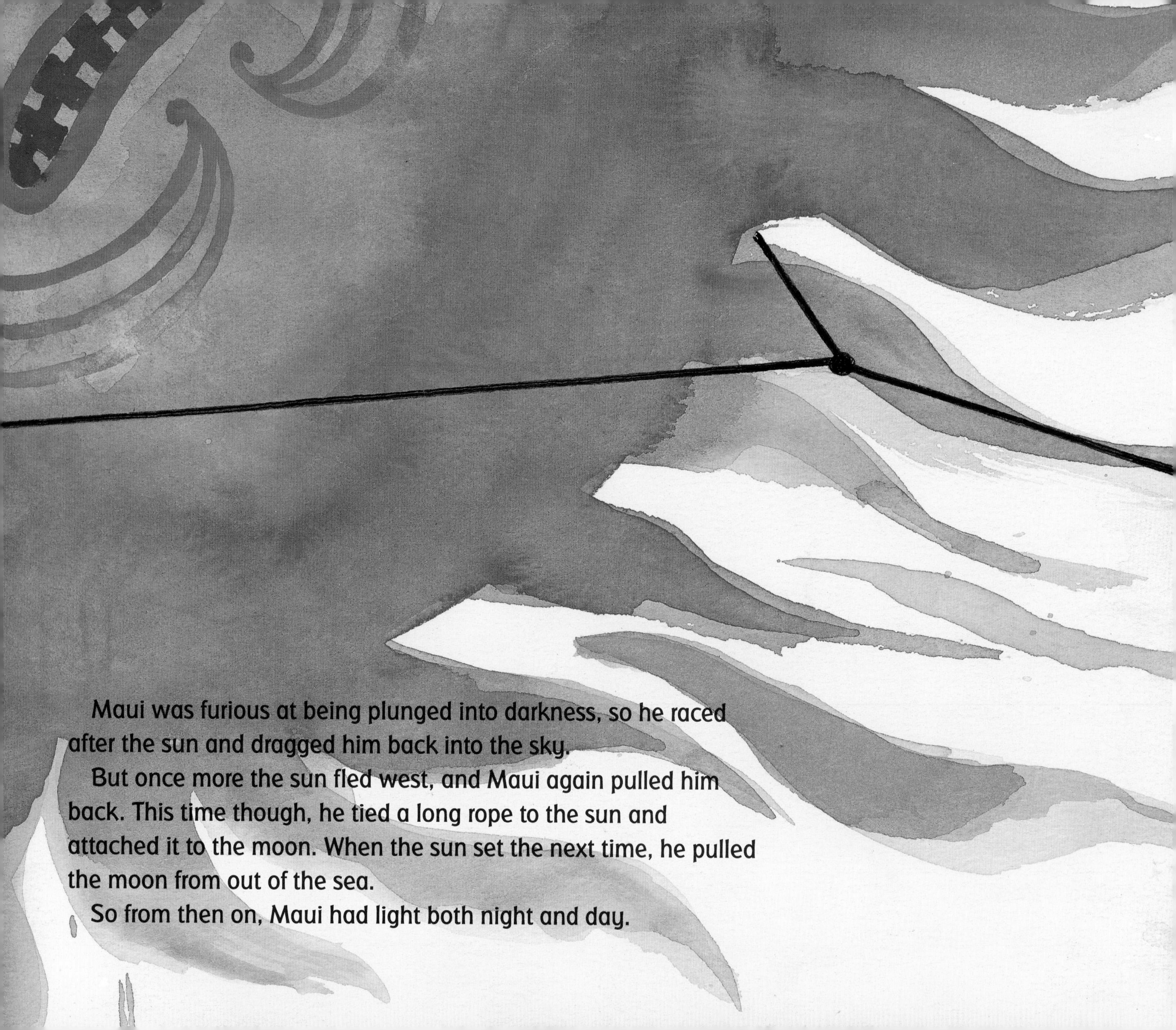

Maui was furious at being plunged into darkness, so he raced after the sun and dragged him back into the sky.

But once more the sun fled west, and Maui again pulled him back. This time though, he tied a long rope to the sun and attached it to the moon. When the sun set the next time, he pulled the moon from out of the sea.

So from then on, Maui had light both night and day.

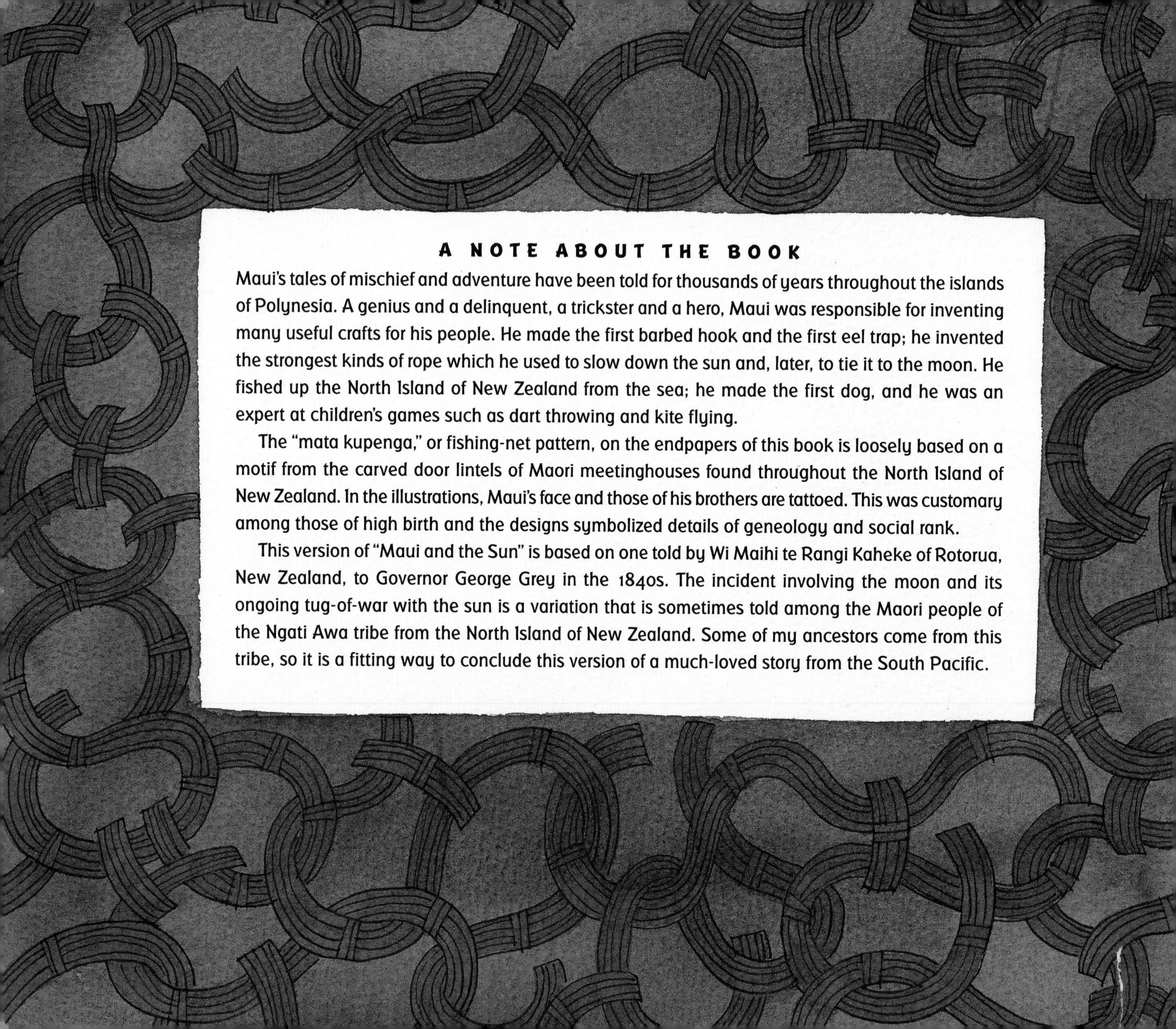

A NOTE ABOUT THE BOOK

Maui's tales of mischief and adventure have been told for thousands of years throughout the islands of Polynesia. A genius and a delinquent, a trickster and a hero, Maui was responsible for inventing many useful crafts for his people. He made the first barbed hook and the first eel trap; he invented the strongest kinds of rope which he used to slow down the sun and, later, to tie it to the moon. He fished up the North Island of New Zealand from the sea; he made the first dog, and he was an expert at children's games such as dart throwing and kite flying.

The "mata kupenga," or fishing-net pattern, on the endpapers of this book is loosely based on a motif from the carved door lintels of Maori meetinghouses found throughout the North Island of New Zealand. In the illustrations, Maui's face and those of his brothers are tattooed. This was customary among those of high birth and the designs symbolized details of geneology and social rank.

This version of "Maui and the Sun" is based on one told by Wi Maihi te Rangi Kaheke of Rotorua, New Zealand, to Governor George Grey in the 1840s. The incident involving the moon and its ongoing tug-of-war with the sun is a variation that is sometimes told among the Maori people of the Ngati Awa tribe from the North Island of New Zealand. Some of my ancestors come from this tribe, so it is a fitting way to conclude this version of a much-loved story from the South Pacific.

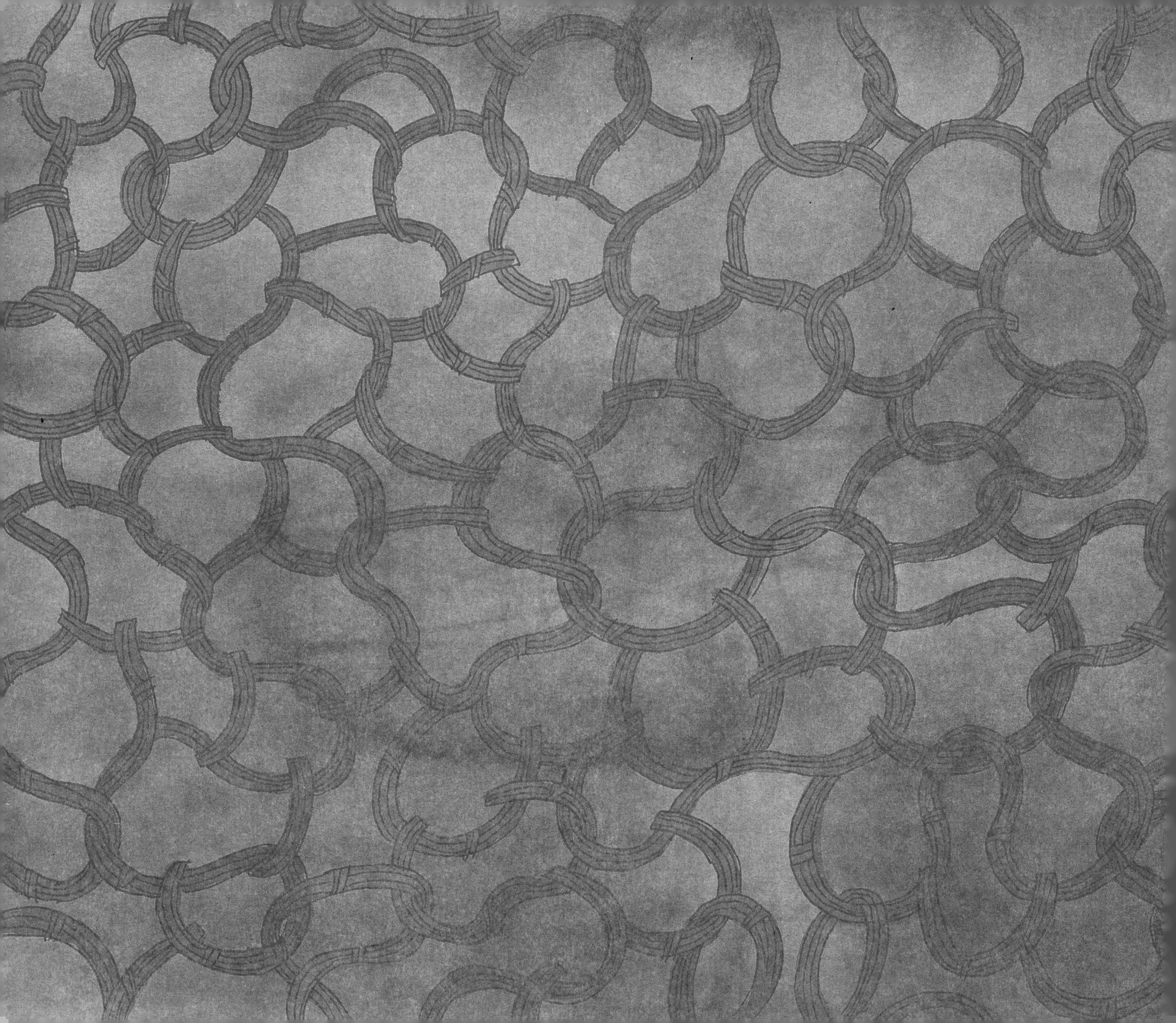